To Caleb + Ava,

I hope you love this little

story ! ♡ love Lori

Bumbles

...saves Naipoki!

By Lori Losch
Illustrations by Pascale Lafond

Dedication

This book is dedicated to every selfless and loving person helping and protecting animals that cannot always help or protect themselves. It is also dedicated to the wonderful people of the David Sheldrick Wildlife Trust who are doing just that. I thank you. Naipoki thanks you. The world thanks you.

Acknowledgements

Thank you Frances Tieulie for helping inspire this second Bumbles book. It was a joy to sit and brainstorm the story together. Thank you Joey Robert Parks for taking the text and adding a little buzzzzzz. I love your editing skills! Thank you Pascale Lafond for bringing the vision for each illustration to life. You nailed it. Thank you TRACares Foundation and Debbie Langenfeld for your financial support. You helped make this book a reality! Most of all, thank you Ken for your unending support. You always encourage my philanthropic adventures and are my biggest cheerleader. I'm forever grateful for you.

In a small village in Africa, there lived a
curious young honeybee named Bumbles.

1

Bumbles loved exploring, so she
flew off in search of an adventure!

Bumbles soared high, very high, above a massive
mountain peak called Kilimanjaro (Kil - ih - man - jar- oh).
"It's beautiful!" said Bumbles.
"It must be the hightest mountain in all of Africa!"

She suddenly heard loud
moaning noises and spotted a
family of elephants far below.
Her eyes darted this
way and that.
Was it the herd of elephants
making the noise?

With a quick swoop,
Bumbles buzzed down
to investigate!

5

"Um, excuuuuuuuuse me!?"
yelled Bumbles to the herd.

6

The animals struggled for a long time,
but they couldn't free the baby
elephant from the mucky
watering hole.
The elephants were very sad.
One by one, they gave up
and walked away.

"Mama elephant!" cried Bumbles.
"Go back! You forgot your baby!"

"Hey, little one," said Bumbles.
"What's your name and
why's your family
leaving you here?"

"I'm Naipoki and I'm too stuck,"
said the elephant. "There's
nothing they can do."

"Well, I'm going to get you
un-stuck!" said Bumbles.

"But you're just a little bee.
My family of big elephants
couldn't even help me.
How in the world can you?"

"Trust me, Naipoki. Just you wait and see!" said Bumbles.

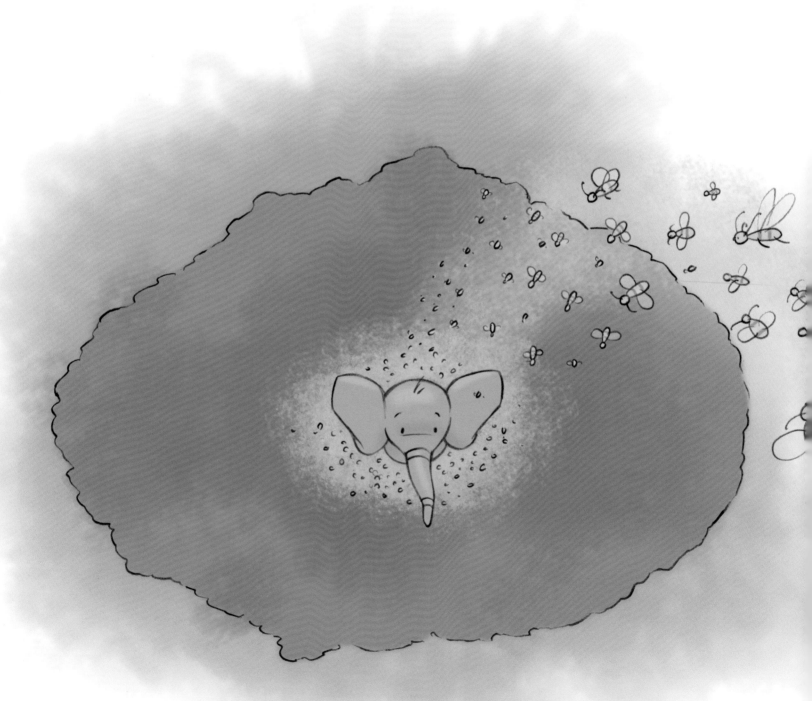

All the honeybees, with their little honeybee-hands
and their little honeybee-feet,
joined together . . . and made . . . a BIG bee blanket!

(Kids . . . you can help them lift her out
by making the sound a flying bumblebee
makes. Ready? One, two, three . . . "Bzzzzzzzzzzz!")

14

"She's way too heavy!" one bee said to Bumbles.

15

"I have an even better idea,"
said Bumbles. "This one
is sure to work!"
With that, Bumbles buzzed
away to find the eagle
she'd seen earlier.

"Excuse me, Mrs. Eagle?" said Bumbles.
"A baby elephant is stuck in a
watering hole. We think your
powerful wings can lift her out.
Would you help us?"

"Caw! Great idea! Caw!
Yes! We can! Caw!"
said Mrs. Eagle.

As Bumbles led the way, Mrs. Eagle cawed
to her friends, "To the watering hole, we fly.
Can we save the baby elephant? We will try!"

When they got to the watering hole, Mrs. Eagle saw a problem.

"How do we hold on to her?" asked Mrs. Eagle.
"Our claws are much too sharp," said one of the eagles.
"You're right," said another. "We'll definitely hurt her."
"Oh dear," said Bumbles. "Let me think."

"Um . . . er . . . e-e-excuse me, Mr. Crocodile?"
said Bumbles to the huge water lizard
with the big scary teeth.
"Our friend is stuck in a watering hole.
We tried a blanket of bees to free her,
but she was too heavy. Some eagles also tried,
but their claws were too sharp.
So, we desperately need your help."

"I dunno," said Mr. Crocodile.
"I'm pretty comfortable here in the shade."

"Please?" said Bumbles.
"Pretty please!?" said Mrs. Eagle.

"All you have to do is lay down next to the baby elephant and we'll do all the work," said Bumbles. "Please?"

"Arggggg! Alright," said the cranky croc.
"Just stop with all the pleases, if you please."

"Push!" cried Bumbles.
"Puuuuuuush!"

The blanket of bees swarmed and buzzed.
The flock of eagles flapped and flew.
Everyone tried to push baby elephant
onto Mr. Crocodile's back.
But she just wouldn't budge.

"I think this is it," said the baby elephant.
"I'm a goner." But Bumbles refused to give up.

She waved "come with me" to the
other bees and they followed her.

"Help! Help!" the men screamed.
They panicked and ran. They flapped
their arms to avoid being stung by the swarm.
To their surprise, the bees didn't sting them at all!

The men saw the baby elephant
stuck in the watering hole. They instantly understood
why the bees had led them there.

The men got to work quickly. They placed long wooden planks beside the baby elephant and carefully tied ropes around her.

"It's going to be okay, Naipoki," said Bumbles.
"Trust me. These men will free you.
When they pull, just put your feet
on the planks and walk out."

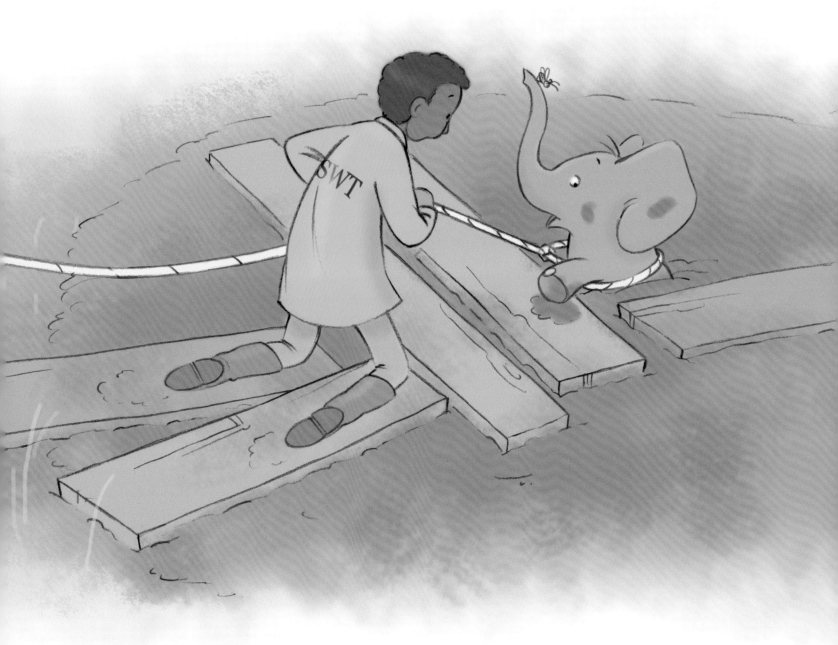

"One, two, three . . . GO!" the men
yelled to the truck driver.

The engine revved loudly. The truck lurched forward.
Little by little, the baby elephant was getting un-stuck.

Then, to everyone's amazement
. . . **POP!**
Out she came.

"Woo hoo! I'm free! Thank you!"
said Naipoki to her new friends.

David Sheldrick
Wildlife Trust

36

"Mama! Mama! You should have seen it!
The bees couldn't do it. The birds couldn't do it.
The crocodile couldn't do it. But all together,
along with these men and their powerful truck,
they saved me!"

About Naipoki

Naipoki is the only elephant at the David Sheldrick Wildlife Trust (DSWT) in Northern Kenya to be rescued *twice* from the same well.

In the early morning of December 13, 2009, the Namunyak Conservancy headquarters learned that three-month old Naipoki had fallen into the well. She was immediately rescued and—after huge efforts to locate her herd—was reunited with her mother on the evening of the 14th.

Sadly, it was reported the next morning that she'd fallen down the same well again. Predators had chewed her trunk and she was in desperate need of milk.

Perhaps the herd she was reunited with was not her own and she'd not been fed? Maybe in her desperation for something to drink she'd fallen into the well? Or conversely, maybe it *was* her herd and she'd simply slipped again into the watering hole they frequent?

Piers and Hilary, advisors to the Namunyak Trust (a trust that looks after the land and wildlife of the Sarara Camp), initiated the second rescue. While they waited for the crew from the DSWT to arrive, Naipoki was returned to their camp in Northern Kenya.

A few hours after the emergency call, the DSWT team arrived at the airstrip to find the little traumatized calf desperately hungry and terribly tired. They fed Naipoki rehydration liquid, which she promptly guzzled, along with two large bottles of milk!

She was loaded onto the plane and strapped in for the journey. With her belly full, she was totally calm and slept most of the flight. On her arrival at the Nairobi DSWT nursery, she was fed again. Her strength began to return. Happily, Naipoki pushed around the loving DSWT elephant keepers, and finally collapsed on the soft hay in her stable for a three-hour nap.

Naipoki was given her name by the people who worked so hard to save her from the well in the Namunyak Conservation area. In the Maa language, Naipoki means 'something painted.' This was also the name of the area where she was reunited with the herd on the evening of December 14th. She came from the exact area as her DSWT nursery mate, Wasin, and the two of them made an endearing pair of miniature elephants. One hopes their friendship will last a lifetime.

Naipoki's story has a happy ending, but many do not. Sadly, countless calves are left to perish. Either they fall into man-made wells or they get stuck in natural watering holes. Many others are orphaned by the ivory-poaching industry.

There are countless such stories of the DSWT and other organizations in the region, rescuing animals which would have otherwise died. I have a huge heart of gratitude for the good people of the DSWT and all those who are rescuing animals globally. They do their work quietly and with no fan-fare. They rescue and help those who can't help themselves. They feed those who can't feed themselves. They protect those who can't protect themselves.

"The greatness of a nation and its moral progress can be judged by the way its animals are treated."
~ Mahatma Gandhi

I thank God for the many people and organizations in this world that are committed to animal welfare. My heart goes out to you all.

About the David Sheldrick Wildlife Trust

Born from one family's passion for Kenya and its wilderness, the DSWT is the most successful orphan-elephant rescue and rehabilitation program in the world today. It's also one of the most pioneering wildlife conservation and habitat protection organizations in East Africa.

It was founded in 1977 by Dr. Dame Daphne Sheldrick D.B.E in honor of her late husband, David Leslie William Sheldrick MBE. He was a famous naturalist and founding warden of Tsavo East National Park. The DSWT claims a rich and deeply rooted family history in wildlife and conservation.

Mission Statement: The David Sheldrick Wildlife Trust embraces all measures that complement the conservation, preservation and protection of wildlife. These include antipoaching; safe guarding the natural environment; enhancing community awareness; addressing animal-welfare issues; providing veterinary assistance to animals in need; and rescuing and hand-rearing elephant and rhino orphans, along with other species that can ultimately enjoy a quality of life in the wild when grown.

At the heart of the DSWT's conservation activities is the Orphans' Project, which has achieved worldwide acclaim through its hugely successful elephant and rhino rescue and rehabilitation program.

The Orphans' Project exists to offer hope for the future of Kenya's threatened elephant and rhino populations as they struggle against the threat of poaching for their ivory and horns, the loss of habitat due to deforestation and drought, and human population pressures and conflict.

The DSWT has successfully hand-raised over 150 infant elephants to date. It has accomplished its long-term conservation priorities by reintegrating former orphans into the wild herds of Tsavo, and many of the DSWT elephants have now raised wild-born calves of their own. This is further testament to the success of the project.

The DSWT has remained true to its principles and ideals, remaining a sustainable and flexible organization. They're guided by experienced and dedicated Trustees and assisted by an Advisory Committee of proactive naturalists with a lifetime of wildlife and environmental experience. The DSWT takes effective action and achieves long-lasting results.

The DSWT is chaired by Daphne Sheldrick and run by Angela Sheldrick, David and Daphne's daughter. Angela has managed the Trust's activities for over a decade. Growing up in Tsavo and later in the Nairobi National Park, she has been part of the Trust's vision from the start and is supported by her husband Robert Carr-Hartley and their boys Taru and Roan, who are equally passionate about Kenya's wildlife and eager to ensure that David and Daphne's legacy continues.

In 2004, the DSWT was granted charitable status by the Charities Commission in the UK. That same year, the Trust attained US Charitable status, further enhancing its corporate funding capability under the guidance of the U.S. Friends of the David Sheldrick Wildlife Trust.

For further information and to donate to this worthy cause, please visit SheldrickWildlifeTrust. org. And to order a copy of Dame Daphne's memoire, *Love, Life, & Elephants: An African Love Story,* visit Amazon.com

About Lori & Bumbles

The idea for the Bumbles the Bee children's book series was born after a recent trip to Zambia. I traveled with two girlfriends, Frances and Suzanne, to bring the ladies living in small villages surrounding Kafakumba (a training center close to Ndola), a skill that could empower them and their families with a new source of income. (You can learn about this adventure in the first book of the Bumbles series: *Bumbles … finds her way home!*) When we returned to North America, we were inspired to write a book to showcase the outstanding work that John and Kendra Enright are doing in Africa.

We then traveled to Kenya to visit Maxwell, Kibo and Kainuk: the rhinos and elephants we sponsored at the DSWT. We were so touched by all they were doing for orphaned and injured rhinos and elephants that another book highlighting that great effort just had to be written. *Bumbles … saves Naipoki!* is the fruit of that inspiration.

We also adopted a few more animals: 10-month-old elephant calf Naipoki—for Lori's mom and for Suzanne's husband; and rhino Solio—for Frances' friend, Lorne.

As I continue traveling and serving in other developing countries, I've had my heart warmed by the outstanding people and organizations doing fabulous things for humanity, animals, and the environment. I considered starting my own charitable organization to spearhead the work globally, but decided I'd rather write books that highlight and support the work others are already doing around the world.

I call it 'sprinkling fairy dust' on these amazing organizations. They deserve it.

It's my hope that each book inspires children and adults alike into taking action: following their passion for service, giving generously to aid those on the front lines, and making the world a better place in ways that only they—you—can.

One such couple, Dwight and Debbie Keller, has done just that. After having been inspired by visits

to Botswana, Uganda, Rwanda, and especially the DSWT in Kenya, they decided to start their own charitable organization focusing on helping orphaned and abused animals. They called it the Keller/Langenfeld Power to Wildlife Foundation. After returning to the States and reading *Bumbles … finds her way home!* they discovered we were kindred spirits and suggested that a book be written based on an elephant rescue. They had no idea that I also support the DSWT and that *Bumbles … saves Naipoki!* had already been written.

They also informed me that they had just adopted an elephant on my and my husband's behalf. Her name was Naipoki! Seriously? There are thousands of animal rescues on the planet and hundreds of thousands of orphans, and they had given us the gift of the same elephant I met, fell in love with, played with, adopted for a family member and had written a book about! This was no coincidence. I'm doing just what I'm meant to be doing. What I love doing. And I hope you join the party!

This synchronicity confirmed for Dwight and Debbie that they are also doing what they are meant to be doing. By following Gandhi's's famous words, to 'be the change you want to see in the world,' they are truly making a difference.

I'm sincerely grateful you've read *Bumbles … saves Naipoki!* to your kids—and to yourself. You are changing lives, as for every 50 copies sold, I am adopting another orphaned elephant or rhino at the DSWT—all thanks to you!
